Beast Quest®

BATTLE OF THE BEASTS

SEPRON
vs
NARGA

With special thanks to Michael Ford

For Will Banks

www.beastquest.co.uk

ORCHARD BOOKS
338 Euston Road, London NW1 3BH
Orchard Books Australia
Level 17/207 Kent St, Sydney, NSW 2000

A Paperback Original
First published in Great Britain in 2013

Beast Quest is a registered trademark of Beast Quest Limited
Series created by Beast Quest Limited, London

Text © Beast Quest Limited 2013
Cover by Steve Sims © Orchard Books 2013
Inside illustrations by Dynamo © Orchard Books 2013

A CIP catalogue record for this book is available from
the British Library.

ISBN 978 1 40832 409 7

3 5 7 9 10 8 6 4 2

Printed in Great Britain by CPI Group (UK) Ltd, Croydon, CR0 4YY

The paper and board used in this paperback are natural recyclable
products made from wood grown in sustainable forests. The
manufacturing processes conform to the environmental regulations of
the country of origin.

Orchard Books is a division of Hachette Children's Books,
an Hachette UK company

www.hachette.co.uk

SEPRON
VS
NARGA

BY ADAM BLADE

ORCHARD

THE

THE FOREST
OF FEAR

WESTERN OCEAN

THE

THE RUBY DESERT

SPIN

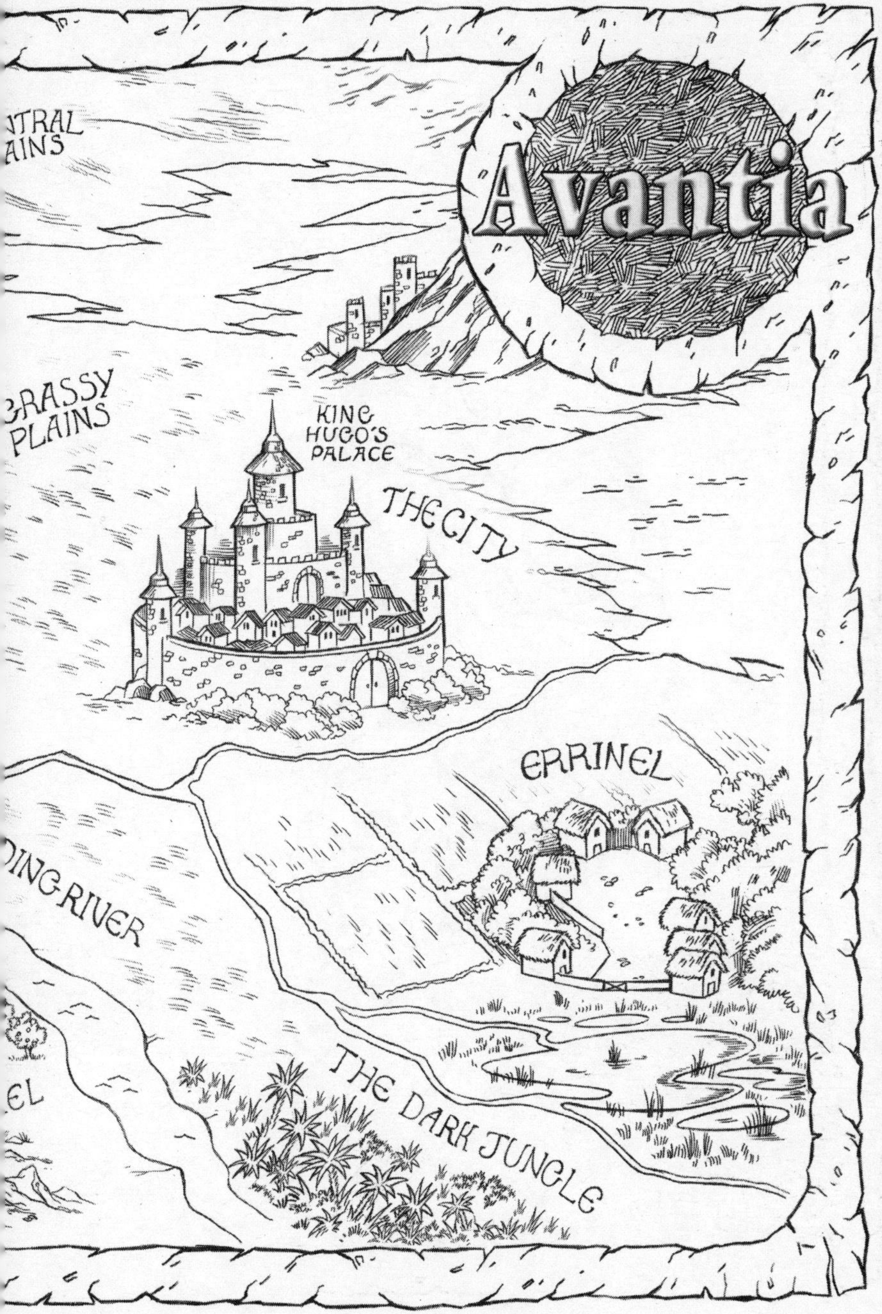

Avantia
NTRAL
AINS
GRASSY
PLAINS
KING
HUGO'S
PALACE
THE CITY
ERRINEL
DING RIVER
EL
THE DARK JUNGLE

Greetings, Will of Shipton-on-Sea!

Word has reached me of your bravery. Are you ready to become a hero?

I am Tom, Master of the Beasts. It is my duty to protect Avantia. But evil never sleeps, and I travel from east to west, north to south, keeping our enemies at bay. So, to help me, I have decided to create a new band of Knights. I want you to be one of them!

Ride swiftly to King Hugo's Palace. There, you will join my Knight Academy, where you will learn the art of combat — and the secrets of the Beasts.

Avantia is counting on you!

Tom

PART ONE

A NEW HERO

CHAPTER ONE

FREYA'S CHALLENGE

Elenna stood at the prow of a small fishing boat, the corners of a fishing net held together in both hands. "Like my uncle Leo used to say, it's all in the way the net is prepared," she said. "If it's folded properly, all you need to do is throw it firmly. Watch!"

She twisted from her hips, flung her arms, and released the net. It opened like a sail, and fell across a patch of

water. The corner weights dragged it
beneath the waves, but Elenna had a
rope attached to the edges, ready to
haul it back in.

"Looks easy enough to me,"
muttered Seb, a dark-haired older boy.
"Even a *girl* can do it."

Will rolled his eyes. Catching fish with a net wasn't easy at all, he knew that well enough. He'd grown up by the sea, diving for oysters in the small hamlet of Shipton. Day after day he'd watched the ships head out at dawn and come back laden with their catches. There weren't many fishermen in his village who knew the waters as well as Lady Elenna, companion to Tom, the Master of the Beasts. Fishing wasn't Elenna's only talent – she was famed for her skill as an archer, too. Even now, out here in the safety of Avantia's Western Ocean, she had her bow slung across her shoulders and a quiver of arrows at her back.

Will glanced across their fleet of six small boats. All of the Knights-in-Training were watching Elenna as she heaved the net in. Even her wolf, Silver, looked on keenly, his paws on the boat's edge and his pink tongue lolling. They'd rowed out from the western shore at dawn and now the coast was just a distant blur above the horizon. Will couldn't help but shiver. The sky was clear at the moment, but if a storm came they'd be in trouble, sailing such fragile vessels so far from home. *Don't be silly,* he told himself. *There's no storm coming today.*

"Caught any sea monsters?" called a voice from one of the other boats. Will turned and saw Tom, his brown hair whipped by a sea breeze and a smile on his face.

Will still couldn't believe he'd been chosen by Tom as a future Knight. What an honour, to learn how to fight alongside a Master of the Beasts!

One day, Will promised himself, *I'll be a great warrior too, and all of Shipton will remember me.*

He wondered if Tom would have chosen him if he'd known about the accident. Will shook the thought away. He couldn't pass up the chance now that he was here.

Elenna tugged the net onto the deck. It writhed with dozens of shining fish.

"We'll eat well tonight," said Will's friend Evan. She'd already completed a special Quest for Tom. Though Will had questioned her about it many times, Evan only gave him a few details. She was far too modest to boast about her triumph. "Right," said Elenna. "Now I want all of you to give it a try. Will, you first."

Will stepped up to the prow beside

her, and took a net from the floor. It was heavier than it looked, but he tried to copy Elenna's movements exactly as he threw it over the water. The net wobbled and unfurled, and landed with a splash. "Good!" said Elenna.

"I don't understand why we're wasting time with this," said Seb. "Catching trout is hardly the same as killing Beasts, is it?"

All the trainees went quiet, looking at each other nervously.

"First of all," said Tom, from his boat, "we never kill Beasts unless we have to. And second, survival is a very important part of a Quest. After all, you can't fight if you're starving, can you?"

Seb blushed and lowered his eyes.

"Carry on, Will," said Elenna.

Will drew in his net, hand over hand. His heart sank with disappointment as it reached the surface. *But how can it be empty? I threw it almost as well as Lady Elenna…*

"Great catch!" said Seb with a sneer. "You're a real natural."

"Strange," said Elenna. "It was a perfect cast." She shot a worried glance to Tom's boat.

As the two boats drew side by side, Tom hopped aboard theirs. He rushed up to Elenna and they began whispering to each other.

Will felt a nudge at his shoulder. "Look!" said Evan, pointing out to sea.

Cutting through the waves was a grand ship – a shallow barge under blue sails bearing a red crescent. The timbers of its hull gleamed with a high polish. At the prow was a figurehead – a woman's body with the roaring head of a lion. Oars carved the water, adding speed to the sails. Will had never seen anything like it in Shipton's harbour. It was a warship, dwarfing Tom's small fishing vessels.

"We're being attacked!" said Seb, his voice cracking with fear.

"It's no enemy," Tom declared. "Those are Gwildor's colours."

Will had never been to Avantia's twin kingdom across the Western Ocean, but he'd heard all manner of strange stories about the place. It was said to be a perfect land, with sparkling blue seas, fields the colour of scattered emeralds, and jungles filled with strange creatures and plants of every hue.

Despite Tom's words, Will couldn't help noticing that the Master of the Beasts had his hand on his sword-hilt, as though ready to fight.

The barge rose and fell across the waves, its oars straining and creaking. Will made out crewmen scurrying over the deck, pulling on ropes or winding winches.

"To starboard!" shouted a woman's

voice. "Bring us closer!"

Then he saw her – a tall figure with long dark hair flowing over the silver plates of her armour. A sword hung sheathed at her side, and she had an oblong shield slung over her shoulder.

"Who's she?" Will asked with a gasp, as the barge drifted alongside.

"That's Freya," said Evan, her eyes bright with excitement. "I've always wanted to see her. She's Tom's mother – one of the bravest warriors in all the known kingdoms."

"One of the bravest *female* warriors," put in Seb. "She wouldn't stand a chance against a *real* knight."

Will ignored him. It was obvious from all the dents and scratches in her armour that Freya had faced many foes. *Seb wouldn't be this confident if he was facing her in the practice yard.*

"Mother!" called Tom. "Thank you for joining us!"

"When I received the wizard's message that you were training your recruits close to my waters, I couldn't let the opportunity pass," said Freya. "You know ocean Quests are my speciality." A mischievous smile broke out over her lips. "Besides, I need to make sure these young warriors are *properly* trained."

Tom grinned. "What do you think, Knights-in-Training? Would you like a lesson with Freya of Gwildor?"

"Yes!" Will cried, along with all the others. Well, almost all of them. Seb was grumbling something under his breath.

"Go ahead then," said Tom to his mother, "but be gentle with them."

From her hip, Freya drew a bone-handled dagger with a long, curved blade. She held it above her head, so all could see. "I won this dagger when I became Mistress of the Beasts," she said. "It's one of my kingdom's greatest treasures. Some say that if the dagger is ever lost, great peril will fall upon Gwildor and her allies."

Will stared at the gleaming blade. He could almost sense the magic in the ancient weapon. *What a thing to own…*

With a flick of her arm, Freya sent the dagger spinning into the ocean between the boats. It landed in the waves with a splash.

A gasp went up through the recruits. Even Elenna's hand shot to her mouth with shock.

"Right," said Freya. "Who among you will retrieve it?"

CHAPTER TWO

THE DEEPEST DIVE

Silence fell over the boats. The dagger had already disappeared beneath the water, and Will imagined it sinking slowly down and down, hundreds of fathoms. He looked around, expecting to see Seb stepping up to volunteer. He was such a glory hunter, and this was his chance to stop whingeing and actually do something. But the older recruit had shrunk to the back of the boat and was looking at his feet.

I'm not surprised he doesn't fancy his chances. Freya has set us an almost impossible task…

Will stared into the black water. When diving for oysters back in Shipton, he could always hold his breath for longer than his friends, and never panicked in the underwater currents as the others did. That was the key to diving. *"Keep calm,"* his father used to tell him, *"and swim steadily. Don't think about the dangers or you'll waste your energy."*

He could almost hear his father's voice in his head, and a wave of grief swept over him. *If it wasn't for me, he might still be alive…*

Before Will knew what he was doing, he stepped forward and held up his hand.

"I volunteer!"

Tom grinned. "A brave decision, Will of Shipton."

"A stupid one, more like," muttered Seb.

Will made his way to the edge of the boat. As he passed Evan, she clapped him on the back. "I'll do my best…" he said, readying himself to jump.

"Wait a moment," said Freya. Will paused. *The longer I delay, the harder it will be!*

He felt a shudder run through his legs. It was just like the accident, all over again…

Freya reached into a bag made of silver net that hung at her waist, and took out a gleaming pearl the size of an apple. It took Will's breath away – he'd seen pearls before, but nothing as large as this. *It must be priceless!*

"This is the magical Pearl of Gwildor," Freya said. "It allows the bearer to breathe beneath the water."

She cast it into the air and Will caught it. The smooth surface was warm in his palm, and scattered the

sunlight in dazzling rays. The other recruits leaned closer, gasping in amazement.

"That's cheating," grumbled Seb. "If I'd known you'd get that pearl, I'd have—"

Freya silenced him with a stern look. "The task is not easy, and every second wasted makes it harder still. Go, Will of Shipton, and good luck."

Tom clapped Will on the back, and Evan called out, "You can do it!"

Will clutched the pearl. Out of habit, he took a deep breath, and jumped from the boat where the dagger had entered the water.

He entered the waves in a perfect dive. The cold gripped him like a freezing fist, but the shock was brief. With one hand holding the pearl, he kicked hard and heaved himself powerfully through the water.

Down, down, down he swam. The waters were dark and gloomy, but the pearl cast an unnatural pale light that made it possible to see a little way ahead. As his throat began to burn, panic crept over Will's heart. What if Freya was wrong about the pearl? What if it worked for others, but not for him? He was too far down to turn back now. His chest was on fire, and he knew that if he opened his mouth now, water would rush in.

What a fool I've been! I'm going to drown! Just like my father…

Memories of the accident flooded back. They'd gone fishing together, as they often had. The sea was calm – there was no reason for either of them to fall overboard. But, while he was at the stern, Will heard his father's cry and the splash of a body hitting the water. He turned around and saw no sign of him. He told himself, over and over again, that his father would pop back up at any moment, with a smile on his face. He was a strong swimmer, so a simple fall into the sea should not be too difficult for him to handle.

But time passed, and his father did not return. At first Will wondered if he was playing a joke, but soon dread crept over his heart. Something was wrong. This was no jape. He dived into the water himself, but it was too late. He found his father eventually, on the seabed, his feet tangled in a net. Will was too late.

It was an accident, the other fishermen said, when they dragged his father's body ashore – just a terrible accident.

But if I hadn't hesitated, Will had thought at the time, *my father might still be alive…*

The last of his breath was spent. When Will could resist no longer, he opened his mouth. But instead of water surging into his throat, his lungs filled with air. The pearl had worked. *I can breathe!*

Will swam on with renewed strength, his fingers gripping the pearl more tightly. *My life depends on it.*

How far down was he? Certainly deeper than he'd ever dived before. Fingers of sunlight reached down from above. Beyond that, darkness seemed to go on forever. But there was not a single fish swimming the depths. How strange! He remembered his empty net.

These waters should be teeming with life, Will thought. *Something is very wrong down here.*

Then he saw the dagger, glinting as it sank through the water. He struck after it, passing the branches of a coral outcrop glimmering red-orange.

Seaweed fluttered, bright green in the
current. Below, the sea dipped past
a huge shelf into blackness. Ignoring
the fear that stole across his skin, Will
kicked harder still, stretching with
his free hand. He couldn't wait to see
Seb's face when he broke the surface
again, clutching the dagger.

He swam past the coral's reaches,

reaching out with both hands. His
fingers brushed the hilt of the dagger.
So close…

"Argh!" Will jerked aside and a
burst of bubbles escaped his lips. A
shape had reared from the depths.
A face with two deep-set eyes and a
scaly snub nose loomed towards him.
It was a giant snake, its neck so long

it stretched off into the ocean's black depths. The snake's red forked tongue flickered between fanged jaws, as if tasting his fear.

Will kicked in the opposite direction, the dagger forgotten. He'd only swum a stroke when a second snake lurched towards him. Fangs snapped in the water, close to his face. Will struck for the surface, swimming harder than he ever had before. When he threw a panicked glance over his shoulder, he saw not two, but five...no, *six* heads in the water. Their coiling necks trailed below, and seemed to join in a single spot.

It's not six snakes, thought Will desperately, as realisation dawned. *It's one Beast with six heads!*

Each of the heads snapped around

to face him. Twelve slitted eyes stared hungrily.

Then they lunged through the water towards him.

CHAPTER THREE

THE GOLDEN GAUNTLET

Will knew he couldn't outpace the
Beast. He swam for the coral forest
and slid between two glowing
branches, feeling a snake-head
surging after him. Slicing under an
arch of coral, he dragged his feet clear
as the fangs snapped. Will pushed
himself deeper into the twisting
branches. The snake heads tried to

follow, but the passages were too narrow and they drew away in one sudden movement.

Has the Beast given up? Will wondered. His knuckles were white as he gripped the pearl and glanced about. Suddenly, the boats – and the other Knights-in-Training – seemed a long way off.

Strands of kelp swayed gently in the water, twice as tall as a man. Will plunged into the slimy tendrils. The Beast passed by, heads probing the water in search of him. Will stayed perfectly still as the lumpy body glided past. *If I leave the shelter of the kelp, I'm a sitting duck... But I have to warn Tom and the others what's down here.*

The great sea monster turned and circled by again. *He knows I'm here*

somewhere. *Perhaps he can smell my fear.*
The six heads all pointed in different
directions, searching out their prey.
One nosed through the kelp, just an
arm's length from Will. His breath
caught in his throat and he waited
until it passed.

It's now or never…

Will pushed off from the seabed,

and heaved with all his might towards the faint daylight above. He didn't even dare to look over his shoulder as he propelled himself to safety, but he could feel the Beast coming after him like a trailing shadow. Soon he saw the dappled outlines of the boats in the water and with a final lunge he broke through the waves.

"Help!" Will shouted. "There's something down there!"

Seb was grinning. "Yes, the *dagger's* down there," he said. "And it looks like you've failed to bring it back."

But Tom wore a worried frown as he reached down to haul Will up into the boat.

"A monster…" Will gasped.

Seb tutted. "What a pathetic excuse—"

Elenna silenced him with a look.

"Tell us what you saw, Will," she said.

Will turned to Freya. "I'm sorry I didn't retrieve your dagger," he said.

"Just describe this Beast," she said. All the playfulness had gone from her face, and for a moment Will felt a shiver of fear as he looked into her hard stare.

Will told them about the creature, about its six heads lined with deadly teeth, and its slitted, glowing eyes.

"Narga!" Tom exclaimed.

Elenna frowned. "But how can that be? You defeated Narga the Sea Monster many Quests ago."

"And yet Will describes him perfectly," said Tom. "The evil magic of Maximus clearly grows stronger."

The rest of the trainees were muttering to one another, and even Seb had lost his smirk. Maximus was the evil son of Malvel, a wizard who had hated Avantia. Malvel had tried and failed to take control of the kingdom many times, but his son was just as determined. He wanted to sit on King Hugo's throne himself and had embarked on an evil plan to avenge his father's death.

Will shuddered. He'd never be able to forget his terror when Maximus snatched the precious gauntlets from the Golden Armour. He could still hear the horrible words of Maximus's curse, echoing around the palace wall:

"Come, cruel magic of Malvel,
Fill these gauntlets with your spell.
Lure two Beasts to deadly battle,
Make them fight with tooth and claw,
'Til one Beast lives and one draws
breath no more."

In the end, Maximus had managed to steal just one of the gauntlets, so he had the power to enslave only one Beast. But one Beast was enough to wreak havoc and destruction across Avantia. When Maximus was controlling a Beast, the only way to stop him was for a Knight to tame a Good Beast, and then lead that Beast in battle. Will glanced at Evan and saw that her face was pale and serious. He knew that she'd already faced such a challenge and only just escaped with her life.

"Do you think Maximus has somehow brought Narga back to life, only to enslave him?" asked Will.

Tom stared into the water. "He's shown himself to be cunning and merciless," he replied. "We have to expect the worst from the son of Malvel. If he now has magic strong enough to bring dead Beasts back to life, that makes him a more dangerous opponent than ever."

Elenna strode across the ship. "We must head for shore," she said. "Surely Maximus has some lair where he's working on his evil magic."

Tom's hand fell to the hilt of his sword and he drew it out a fraction. "If Maximus had such a base, I'm sure the Circle of Wizards would have rooted it out. I wish I could face Malvel's son once and for all."

"Patience, my son," said Freya, "that day will come. Have faith in your recruits. The second gauntlet will choose Maximus's adversary."

Tom let his sword slide back into its sheath. "You're right." He fished in the bag at his waist and drew out

the golden gauntlet. Will sucked in a breath as it sparkled in the sun.

"Who will be Avantia's next champion?" asked Tom. "Who will face Maximus and Narga?"

CHOOSING A CHAMPION

"At last!" said Seb, leaping forward.
"A *real* battle rather than silly games.
This one has *got* to be my Quest!" He
snatched the gauntlet off Tom. "I'll
show Narg— Argh!"

The gauntlet leapt out of Seb's
hand, flipped over in the air and
shoved him in the chest, sending him
stumbling over a rowing bench. He

landed hard on his backside, the other recruits breaking into laughter as the gauntlet dropped into the bottom of the boat.

"The gauntlet chooses its own champion," said Tom with a smile. "And sadly, Sebastian, it has not chosen you this time."

A blush crept up Seb's cheeks. "So be it," he grumbled. "Let someone else get themselves killed..."

Will stooped to pick up the gauntlet. "Here," he said, offering it back to Tom.

Strange, thought Will. *It feels as light as a feather.*

The gold sparkled brighter in his hand.

Evan grinned at him. "Try it on," she whispered.

Will looked uncertainly at Tom,

who nodded. He slid his fingers inside the gauntlet. The metal shrank and closed snugly over his hand.

"Will of Shipton," said Tom, "this Quest is yours."

Will gazed at the gauntlet in wonder, flexing his fingers. "A Quest? *Me?*"

"*Him?*" said Seb.

A cry on the other side of the boat drew everyone's attention. One of the recruits was pointing to a patch of water, which swirled around and around like a tiny whirlpool.

Will's heart leapt into his throat. *Has Narga returned already?*

But a shape appeared *above* the water, as if forming out of mist. Slowly, it took on the form of a young man in a purple velvet robe and floppy hat.

"Daltec!" said Elenna.

"Greetings, trainees!" said the Good Wizard. "I come to— Oh!" He glanced down, then frowned. His robes were trailing in the seawater, so he hoisted them up and stepped, dripping, into the boat. "I still haven't got the hang of this long-distance travel," he muttered.

"Narga is here," said Tom. "The gauntlet has chosen Will of Shipton as our next champion."

Daltec opened his arms in front of him and immediately a book appeared in his hands. Its leather binding was stained and worn.

The Book of the Beasts, Will read in gold lettering on the cover.

"Come, Will," said Tom, taking the book. "You must choose a Beast to help you do battle with Narga."

Will stood alongside his hero, and opened the book. He could feel its magic tingling through his fingertips. The first page he turned to showed Koldo the Arctic Warrior, a giant made of ice. *He won't do for a water battle*, Will thought. Next he came across Grashkor the Beast Guard, but the book said he was confined to a prison called the Chamber of Pain.

"Keep looking," said Tom.

Will turned the page and his heart jolted with fear. The new page showed a sea serpent with a frilled head and bright green scales.

"Sepron," said Tom. "He's the mightiest of the sea Beasts."

"And he's not far away, either,"

added Freya. "He lives here, in Avantia's Western Ocean."

"But it will take a strong heart to tame him," counselled Elenna.

Will stared at the fearsome Beast. *How can I tackle a creature like that? I couldn't even save my father from drowning.*

His father's voice filled his head again. *"Don't think about the dangers, son."*

"I choose Sepron!" Will said.

"A wise decision," said Tom. "Now, every Quester needs a companion." He cast a grin towards Elenna. "Sometimes a friend fighting by your side can mean the difference between life and death. Evan, you have completed your own Quest already. You will go with Will."

Evan stepped forward, her face

glowing with pride. "It would be an honour!"

"When's it my turn?" demanded Seb, with a sulk. "It's always—"

Freya silenced him with a glare, then turned to the wizard. "Daltec, do you have a map to help our young heroes?"

The wizard was still wringing out the bottom of his robe. "I'm afraid not, my lady," he said. "Not even the greatest of wizards has ever been able to chart the depths of the ocean."

"But how will I find Sepron?" asked Will. *And it's not likely that Narga will stay put…*

Seb chuckled. "Not so confident, now, are you?" he muttered.

Tom laid a hand on Will's shoulder. "I always found it was best to trust my instincts," he said.

Will nodded. *I should have trusted my instincts that day too – I knew that something was wrong.* He glanced at Evan. "We won't fail," he said.

"Good," said Tom, "because all Avantia is depending on you."

CHAPTER FIVE

HUNTING NARGA

Tom, Elenna and Will walked to the prow of the boat and stared into the water. *Maximus's Beast is down there somewhere. But first, I need to find Sepron and tame him.*

"Wait a moment," said Daltec the wizard. "No warrior can undertake a Quest without weapons." He rubbed his hands together, then raised his palms and recited:

*"Protect these heroes from all harm.
Grant our Questers mighty arms."*

Sparks flashed between the wizard's
palms and floated towards Will. As
they faded, he saw a trident in his
gauntleted hand. Its twisted shaft
shone gold, ending in three mighty

prongs like daggers. Their sharp points looked deadly. From Will's belt hung a glittering net. He could see at once that the strands were made not of rope, but metal as fine as thread. It weighed next to nothing.

But will it be strong enough to snare a Beast? he wondered.

He looked at Evan and saw that she clutched a shield and spear, the weapons she'd used on her own Quest.

Will hoisted the trident above his shoulder, testing its balance.

"Good luck, fisherboy," sneered Seb.

"There's one more thing," said Freya. "Hand it over, Seb."

The older boy spread his arms and shrugged. "What are you talking about?"

Freya calmly jumped from the prow of her boat, landing beside Seb and holding out her hand. "You know what."

Seb cowered backwards, but reached into his tunic and took out the pearl of Gwildor.

"Thief!" gasped Evan.

He must have taken it when Tom helped

me out of the water, Will thought.

"It was just a joke," said Seb. "I was going to give it back!"

"Really?" said Freya.

"Everyone gets to go on adventures apart from me," whined Seb.

"You'll get your turn," said Tom, "*when* the gauntlet decides you're ready."

Seb scowled and turned away.

Freya held out the pearl towards Daltec, who reached and touched it with his fingers. His lips moved in a spell that Will couldn't hear, but the pearl sparkled red, then green, then blue, then faded to silvery-white once more. Freya handed the pearl to Will.

"I've blessed the pearl with extra magic," said Daltec. "It won't last for long, but you should both be able to breathe underwater as long as one of you is holding the pearl, and you don't stray too far apart. It will also let you speak to one another beneath the waves."

"Thank you," said Will, slipping the precious pearl into his pocket. He faced Evan. "Ready?"

"As I'll ever be," she said. Together they placed their feet on the boat's edge.

"Good luck, Questers!" said Tom.

The rest of the crew cheered and stamped their feet on the timbers.

Will lifted the trident, and leapt off the boat. He entered the water with barely a splash and through the rising bubbles he saw Evan at his side. Her cheeks were puffed out.

"Just breathe," said Will, amazed that he could hear his own voice in the water.

Evan opened her mouth, then grinned widely. "This is amazing!" she said.

They swam side by side, further into the ocean depths. *Trust my instincts, Tom said.* But Will's instincts were not telling him anything yet. They passed the coral shelf where he'd seen Narga before, but there was no sign of the six-headed Beast.

"I don't see any sea creatures at all," said Evan. "That's not right, is it?"

"It was the same when I was swimming after the dagger," said Will. "Narga must have scared them all off."

"Which means the Beast is close," said Evan, scanning left and right.

Beyond the coral, Will saw the seabed far below, strewn with weeds and boulders, but not even one scuttling crab. "I don't like this," he said. "It's too quiet."

Evan gripped his arm and pointed. Will saw it too – a stream of bubbles, rising ahead. He followed them down to the sea floor, and spotted a dark shadow. *Narga?*

Will's heart began to thump in his chest, and he brandished his trident ahead of him as they swam closer.

But it wasn't the Sea Beast. The shadow was actually the mouth of a cave, and the bubbles were emerging from it.

"Something's inside," Evan whispered. "Something *alive*!"

The water felt suddenly cold to Will, but that might just have been because of the chill in his blood. "Elenna reckoned Maximus must have a lair where he was working on his magic," he said. "What if it's underwater?"

"That makes sense," Evan replied, "since it's a water Beast that he's brought back to life."

"There's only one way to find out," Will said. *I can't turn back now. Tom's depending on me…*

Steeling himself with a deep breath, Will kicked towards the cave.

CHAPTER SIX

A TIGHT SQUEEZE

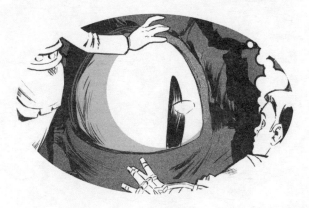

As they reached the cave mouth, Will saw that the bubbles were large, each bigger than his fist. "Whatever is breathing down there is massive," he said to Evan. "We should be careful."

He peered around the edge of the cave entrance but he couldn't see a thing in the darkness. The cave mouth was only just wide enough for them to slip inside, shoulder to shoulder.

Will felt something warm in his
pocket, and drew out the pearl of
Gwildor. It was glowing pale white.

Evan grinned. "I've got an idea."

She took her shield off her shoulder
and held it over the cave entrance.

"Bring the pearl closer," she said.

Will did as she asked. The light from

the pearl reflected off the polished surface of the shield, casting rays into the gloom of the cave. All Will could see was a curved passageway spiralling into blackness.

"I guess we should follow the bubbles," he said. "I'll go first."

The walls of the passageway were bare rock, worn smooth. If something were to attack them in here, it would be hard to manoeuvre. Will checked back to make sure Evan was still with him. The light from the pearl threw her shadow on the wall behind and her eyes were wide open and alert.

The passage reached a fork, branching into two narrower tunnels. Will wasn't sure which to follow at first, but then another stream of bubbles trickled from the left one.

"This way," he said.

There were more forks, and the passages sometimes broke into three or four different tunnels, branching up and down, left and right. Some tunnels doubled back, and soon Will lost track of which way the surface was. "Trust your instincts," he muttered to himself. He followed the bubbles.

Don't think about the dangers, or you'll waste energy.

But a sense of dread was stealing over his heart.

If the pearl's light goes out, we'll be lost down here.

He decided not to voice his fears, but he suspected Evan was probably thinking the same thing.

Then the bubbles ceased. Will stopped, treading water, waiting for a sign to follow. But none came.

"We have to keep going," said Evan.

"We've come too far to turn back."

She's right. The water grew colder still as they followed the tunnel. *Perhaps my instincts were wrong after all,* thought Will.

But then the tunnel began to widen. Will swam faster, sure they were about to uncover Maximus's lair. Then the tunnel halted at a wall of stone covered in green moss-stained rock. A few fronds of seaweed waved gently in the water.

"Dead end," said Evan.

"It can't be!" said Will. "The bubbles *must* have been coming from here."

He slapped the stone in frustration.

The stone moved a fraction.

"Huh?" said Evan. She touched the stone more gently, running her fingers across it. "It feels warm..."

And now, as Will looked closer, it

didn't look like stone at all. The wall shifted slightly again, and flexed like scales under the light of the pearl. Will recognised their colour from *The Book of the Beasts*.

"I think we've found Sepron!" he said.

With a roar that shook Will's bones, the wall seemed to slide away under his hand and a coil of scaled flesh slipped past. Through a gap, he saw more of the sea serpent writhing within a cave beyond. His coils were tightly wound, and some of his scales had been torn away by the rough rock. What Will had thought was seaweed was actually the green crest along the Beast's spine.

"What's he doing down here?" asked Evan.

"He's trapped!" said Will. "It looks

like he wants to escape."

Sepron's body jerked and thumped against the cave walls, and his grunts of pain made the water tremble.

"Poor Sepron!" said Evan. "On my Quest, I tamed Tagus the Horse-Man by removing a stone from his hoof. Maybe you need to help Sepron, too."

"Good thinking," said Will. *But how?*

Sepron's body was grinding against the inside of the cave, and Will laid his hands on the thick scales. "We'll find a way to help you, I promise," he said. He turned to Evan. "Let's retrace our path – one of the other tunnels might lead to a way out."

They swam back to the last fork and took the other route. This passage was pockmarked with holes in the wall, and Sepron's thick hide filled every one. Will was starting to lose

hope, when one of the patches of scale
opened to reveal a slitted eye larger
than Evan's shield. The black pupil
shrank as it focused on Will and his

companion. The eye was bloodshot, and another roar shook the tunnel. Will heard teeth gnashing, grinding like rocks smashed together.

"I know you're angry," said Will, "but Tom sent us down here to help."

"I don't understand," said Evan, keeping a cautious distance from the raging eye. "These tunnels seem to fit around Sepron's body exactly. How did a Beast so clever end up in such a tight spot?"

"Maybe he didn't," said Will. "Perhaps he was trapped."

"You mean…"

"I think Maximus built this cave system around him," said Will, his anger rising. "He must have known Sepron was the only Beast who could take on Narga."

"Then we need to set him free as

quickly as we can," said Evan.

Will scanned around him and saw what he was looking for. Further into the tunnel, where Sepron's scales were pressed right up against the cavern wall, a large rock was wobbling slightly. "Over there," said Will. "It looks loose!"

They swam to the boulder, and Will jabbed his trident beneath the base. "Help me," he said.

Evan angled her spear-point into the gap beside Will's trident. Will leant on the golden shaft and tried to wiggle it like a lever. "If we can collapse the caves, we can free Sepron," he said with a grimace.

Evan heaved on her spear too and the rock shifted a little.

"Keep going!" Will urged her.

As he worked the trident back

and forth, he could feel the boulder loosening. Little rocks tumbled from the tunnel roof and a low rumble filled the water. Sepron bellowed and threw his weight against the walls. *He can taste his freedom*, thought Will. *We're nearly there.*

"It's working!" said Evan. Then the rock toppled outwards and hit the ground with a thump.

Larger sections of the tunnel began to dislodge and fall. Will had to jerk back to avoid being crushed. Evan withdrew her spear as the wall crashed down and a shockwave gripped them, hurling them across the cave. Will saw clear water beyond.

"We'd better get out of here!" he said.

The rumble of collapsing stone

became a deafening roar, and debris
and splinters of rock filled the water.
Will pulled himself up with powerful
strokes, but felt his lungs suddenly
start to burn. *I can't breathe.* He looked
down and saw Evan clutching at her
throat, her eyes wide with fear.

The pearl…

Will's hand shot to his pocket, but it

was empty.

I must have dropped it. It must be buried amid the ruins of the cave.

There was no chance of recovering it now.

We're drowning… just like my father!

CHAPTER SEVEN

IN THE BEAST'S COILS

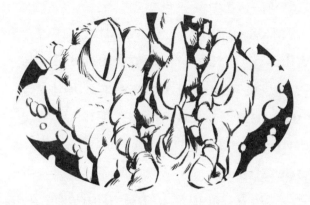

Fear clutched Will's heart and squeezed. *But wait...* There really *was* something gripping him around the chest! Sepron's coils wrapped tightly under his arms and dragged him through the water. Black spots appeared before Will's eyes, but through the bubbles he saw Evan, also held fast in a loop of green scales.

Just a bit more pressure, and Will knew his ribcage would collapse.

Sepron's free, but he's going to crush us. Maybe he thinks we're the ones who trapped him…

Waves of dizziness washed over Will. Would Sepron squeeze his life away, or would the water flood his lungs first? Then he saw the ocean getting lighter around them, and he understood.

He's helping us! Taking us up! Hold on, Evan. Hold on just a little longer.

They broke through the surface and Will sucked in great lungfuls of air. The coils released him, and he saw Evan bobbing in the water too, spluttering up a mouthful of seawater.

Sepron's huge back curled over the waves and his head turned, dripping,

to face them. Great fronds of scaled
flesh hung from his long jaw.

"Thank you!" gasped Will.

A voice inside his head replied: *No,
thank* you, *Will of Shipton – for rescuing
me from my prison.*

Will's face broke into a smile. "I can hear the Beast!" he said to Evan.

Evan grinned too. "That's what happened with Tagus. You've tamed him, Will!"

Sepron roared and dipped his head again, sending up a wave. His vast body, which would dwarf even Freya's barge, arched over the water in a looping coil, and finally his tail slipped out of sight.

"What now?" asked Evan. "Without the pearl we can't even go back underwater."

Will's sense of triumph seeped away. "It's my fault," he said. "I must have dropped it when we were loosening the boulder."

"Can you find it again?" asked Evan.

Will shook his head sadly. "It's

too deep here. It's not like diving for oysters – the pearl could be hidden under mountains of rock by now."

We'll have to swim back to the ship and admit defeat. Narga and Maximus have won...

Water showered over them as Sepron burst from the waves again. He faced Will and opened his jaws wide. Sitting on the end of his tongue, framed by teeth like curved swords, was the pearl of Gwildor.

"Yes!" said Evan, punching the air. "The Quest isn't over yet!"

Sepron leaned so close to Will that he could smell the rotten stink of fish on his breath. *Those teeth could grind me into a paste,* Will thought, *but I've got to trust him.* Trying not to inhale, he reached inside the Beast's mouth, past the deadly teeth, and grabbed the pearl.

Once it was safely stowed back in his pocket, Will stroked Sepron's nose with the golden gauntlet. "We'll need your help," he said. "We need to scour the ocean and find Narga."

I am with you on your Quest, Sepron replied.

The mighty sea serpent let his head drop so it was resting on the surface of the water. Will swam behind it, and gripped the tough scales on his neck. He heaved himself up on the Beast's back. Evan scrambled up behind him. "He's a lot bigger than Tagus," she said.

"Hold on tight!" said Will. "It's time to hunt Narga!"

Sepron rose above the waves with a mighty roar, then crashed beneath the water again. Will blinked through a swarm of bubbles, his knuckles

white where he gripped the sea
serpent's scales. He felt Evan's hands
clutching his tunic as they plunged
deeper and deeper into the water.

"Keep a lookout!" he called to Evan.

The water rushed through his hair
and clothes as Sepron cut through

the buffeting currents. *No ship could travel this fast*, Will thought. Twice the sea serpent jerked into a change of direction and nearly threw Will off, but each time he managed to cling on. The seabed swept past in a blur.

Evan shouted, "Over there!" and Will's eyes tracked her pointing finger. It wasn't Narga, but a shoal of slender silvery fish, all swimming in the same direction like a flight of arrows.

Will tugged on Sepron's scales and the sea serpent slowed and steered towards the shoal.

"They're the first fish we've seen for ages," said Evan.

"And there are more!" said Will.

Behind the shoal came a school of small sharks, and with them hundreds of brightly coloured

parrotfish. *How odd*, thought Will.
*Why aren't the sharks attacking their
prey?*

Other species swam past, too – sea
trout, rays and cuttlefish, all heading
in exactly the same direction. None
seemed interested in one another.
None were chasing or fleeing the
others. Squid of all sizes pulsed in
their wake.

"It's like they're being drawn by
something," said Evan.

"Magic," said Will, grimly. "And
that only means one thing: Narga."
He patted the side of Sepron's neck.
"Follow them!"

The sea serpent turned and set off
after the fish with a flick of his long
tail. Soon a shape loomed through
the water ahead. It wasn't moving,
though. *So it can't be Narga*, Will told

himself.

As they drew nearer, Will made
out a domed structure made of stone
and tightly knitted coral branches. It
wasn't natural, he could see that –
someone had *built* it.

As the fish reached the dome, they
broke into wild swirls, swimming

around its edge as if mesmerised.

"Narga must be inside," whispered Evan.

Sepron took them right over the centre of the strange underwater building, and Will spied a small hole in the top. *Not wide enough for a Beast to enter,* he thought.

They slipped off the sea serpent's broad back. "You stay here," Will said to Sepron. *If I can prevent the Beasts from fighting, I will – even if it means Evan and me taking on Narga alone.*

The fish continued their dance, faster and faster around the dome.

Will forced a path through the opening, and Evan joined him to peer over the rim.

But it wasn't Narga that greeted Will's eyes.

It was Maximus!

PART TWO

BATTLE BEGINS

CHAPTER ONE

MAXIMUS'S LAIR

In the centre of the chamber, Malvel's son sat on a tall throne made of long white whalebones. Half a curved, broken ribcage reached over the top of him, and his feet rested on the whale's bleached skull. On one hand, Maximus wore the second golden gauntlet. He flexed his fist.

"How much longer?" he said, scowling sullenly.

At first Will thought that Malvel's son had seen their hiding place and was speaking to him, but it was another voice that replied – a girl's voice.

"Didn't your father teach you patience?"

Will leaned further over and saw a girl of around the same age as Maximus. She wore a black tunic fastened right up to her neck with silver toggles, and a black cloak over the top. Silver thread marked the symbol of a Beast's skull and crossbones on the cloak's back, and hair as red as fresh blood cascaded over her shoulders.

"Ria!" whispered Will.

Evan looked at him, with a confused frown.

"My uncle used to tell me stories at

the shipyard," Will explained. "One was about a Pirate King called Sanpao who flew a symbol like that on his mast. He had a child called Ria with an Evil Sorceress called Kensa. That must be her!"

The black-clad girl was pouring a flask of bright green liquid into a cauldron. It smoked and hissed, and a cruel smile spread over her lips.

What evil magic is she practising? Will wondered. *And why has she teamed up with Maximus?*

As the boy wizard slid off his throne, Will realised there was something very strange about the chamber. "Maximus is walking!" he said. "The cave is filled with air, not water!"

Evan nodded. "He must be using powerful magic."

"My father was not a patient man," said Maximus below them. He drew his sword a fraction. "He killed people who made him wait too long."

Ria cackled. "Well, I warn you, son of Malvel. If you try to harm me, this

chamber will be your watery grave."
She took another flask from the
table – it contained what looked like
frogspawn.

"Eugh! What's that?" asked
Maximus.

"Eggs of the First Beast," said Ria.
"A very important ingredient for our
plans."

"Don't be foolish!" said Maximus.
"The First Beast was Anoret, and she
was buried in the Stonewin Volcano
four hundred years ago!"

"Don't doubt me, conjuror,"
snapped Ria. "My father gave them to
me. Watch."

She let the eggs splash into the
cauldron, and around the edge of the
chamber, images flickered into life.
Will recognised creatures from *The
Book of the Beasts* – Claw the Giant

Monkey, Stealth the Ghost Panther
and dozens more.

"Evil Beasts!" Evan hissed.
"Maximus must be planning to bring
them *all* back to life, just like he did
Narga!"

Will shuddered. "We have to stop
him. Let's find a way in."

They swam away from their spy-
hole, following the outer wall of

the chamber closely. Sepron's dark silhouette lurked above them in the water.

We might need you soon, Will thought.

In many places they could see through gaps in the rocks and coral, but none of the openings was large enough to enter by. The fish attracted to the lair swirled and swarmed around them. Most were just a nuisance, but Will kept his trident ready in case a shark got too close. He wondered if they should swim back to Tom and Elenna. They needed to be warned about what Malvel's son was planning – and that he had a new assistant.

But if we swim away now, it might be too late by the time we return with help.

He'd waited too long to act when his father fell into the sea.

Evan and I have to deal with Maximus and Ria ourselves. Now.

Evan was waving her arms frantically, beckoning him lower down the curved wall of the underwater lair, close to where it met the seabed. Will swam to her and saw a gap in the coral just wide enough for them to squeeze through. Tucking his trident close against his body, Will went first.

He reached a wall made from a clear, jelly-like substance. *This must be what is keeping the water out*, he thought. He pushed his hand through, then his head, and fell into a low chamber. Air rushed into his lungs and he stood up gingerly. The jelly wall had sealed behind him. The cave was filled with giant clam shells, littering the floor in ankle-deep

water. At the far side was an archway.

That must lead to where Maximus and Ria are, Will thought.

Evan pushed through the jelly wall behind him, and stepped into the cavern. "Evil magic," she said, pressing the sticky goo with her fingers.

"That way," said Will, pointing to the arch. "Stay quiet!"

The clam shells were deadly still, like a hundred open mouths, some reaching as high as Will's waist. Will picked his way between them. He was almost at the arch, when a sudden thought hit him:

What if the clams are enchanted too, like the fish outside…

He turned to warn Evan. She was steadying herself against one of the shells. "Be careful of—"

The clam shifted and her hand slipped. "Argh!" she cried, as both halves of the shell snapped together to clamp over her wrist. Her face twisted with pain and she tried to tug her arm free. "Help me!"

Maximus's voice rang out. "Who dares trespass in my lair?"

CHAPTER TWO

BEAST PREY

Will put a finger to his lips. He thought about hiding, but where could he go? Evan was trapped, and he couldn't leave her.

Time to face our enemy.

Maximus appeared in the archway, his gauntleted hand glinting as it clutched a furled whip. His eyes fell upon Will's gauntlet, and a smile broke across his face.

"It looks like Tom's found another
so-called *champion* to face me," he
said. He unfurled the whip and lashed
it towards Evan. Flames licked the air
where it cracked. "And I can't say it's a
pleasure to see *you* again."

Evan fought to free herself from the
clam shell, but Will could see that her
arm was held fast. Maximus flicked the
whip again, and Will jabbed with his

trident to deflect the blow. The leather caught the prongs with a snap, and bitter smoke drifted through the air.

"Leave her alone!" said Will, tearing his trident free. He jammed the tip into the hinge of the clam and tried to prise it open.

"Run!" said Evan. "Get yourself to safety."

Will ignored her. There was no way he would abandon a fellow Quester.

"Yes, run away, boy," said Maximus. "Evan was lucky last time, but I am more powerful now." He raised his whip again, and sparks fizzed along its length.

Will waited for the blow to fall.

"Wait!" said Ria. The young witch appeared beside Maximus in the archway. "Don't kill them just yet," she said. In her hand, she held a clear vial filled with a turquoise liquid. "These two will be perfect test subjects for our new potion, don't you think?"

Maximus coiled up his whip with a cruel smile.

"Good idea," he said. "They can die nice and slowly."

Will leaned all his weight against the trident's shaft, desperate to force the clam open, but fell back, panting. *It's no use – I can't free Evan.*

Ria held the vial in front of her, and reached into her cloak. "Now for the final ingredient," she muttered. She took out a small golden pot, no larger than a thimble. Opening the lid with her fingernail, she poured a stream of fine white powder into the vial. The liquid changed colour again, becoming pale blue like a winter sky.

Maximus rubbed his hands

together. "You two should feel honoured to be part of my new experiment," he said.

"*Our* new experiment," said Ria. "Maximus, helmets please."

Maximus grinned, and muttered a spell. As Will watched, strange transparent bubbles formed over his enemies' heads.

Maximus lifted both hands, one bare and the other wearing the gauntlet. Lightning bolts shot from both, smashing into the domed roof. The coral and rock seemed to dissolve before Will's eyes and water rushed into the chamber, streaming down the walls and welling up around Will's knees, then over his chest and head. But even if Evan was still trapped, the pearl of Gwildor would at least allow them to breathe...

And Maximus and Ria, too.

"Will, look!" said Evan.

She was pointing at what had once been the roof of the chamber, now completely gone. In its place, Narga lurked in the open water. Seeing his monstrous form all at once, Will couldn't help trembling. The Beast's body was the colour of bright green

seaweed, marked with bulbous red boils. Thousands of fish darted between his writhing necks, twisting out of the way as he snapped at them with six sets of razor-sharp jaws.

We need you now, Sepron, thought Will. *I hope you can still hear me…*

"Now for the finishing touch," said Maximus. He held out his gauntleted hand. Ria handed him the vial, and Maximus tipped it upside down.

The blue liquid escaped and formed a cloud in the water, and Maximus chanted:

"Make this Beast more deadly still,
For now, at last, it's time to kill!"

The liquid shot upwards in the shape of six darts, and each flowed into one of Narga's mouths. The Beast writhed as though he was in pain. Light the colour of sapphires pulsed down the Beast's necks like waves, along his body and tail. A flash blinded Will for a moment and he threw up an arm to cover his face.

When the light faded, Will blinked away the spots behind his eyes.

"It worked!" Ria screeched.

Will stared up at Narga and saw that something had changed. Where his tail had ended in a paddle-like fin, now it curled into the shape of a fleshy sickle.

"They're changing the Beast!" said Evan.

"And making it even harder for us to battle," said Will.

Maximus kicked off from the chamber floor, and swam up to Narga. He threw his leg over the

Beast's back, where his necks joined
together, then drew his whip again.
As he lifted it, the strands magically
wrapped around the Beast's necks,
like leashes. Then he pointed with his

gauntlet at Will and Evan.

"Narga!" he roared. "Why not try out your new tail on these two?"

The Beast's six heads moved as one, and his slitted red eyes rested on them. Six tongues flickered out.

"Narga can taste their fear!" cackled Ria.

Will's heart was pounding. Evan was trapped, and Sepron nowhere to be seen. Inside his head, Will urged, *Come to us!*

He brandished his trident in front of him, waiting for Narga to attack.

We need you now, Sepron!

CHAPTER THREE

BEAST VS BEAST

Narga's heads dipped as one and the Beast swooped down into the cave. Will tried to watch each of the heads, waiting for the snapping jaws to strike. He almost didn't see the tail until too late, sweeping through the water at high speed.

He swung his trident to defend himself, and Narga's sickle caught between two of its prongs. The blow almost took Will's arm off, but he gritted his teeth and held on. Narga pulled back his tail and swiped again. This time Will only managed to deflect the blow and the sickle's tip slashed his shoulder. He winced as his blood clouded in the water.

Narga roared in triumph and twisted to strike once more. The sickle swung towards Will's neck, but Evan's spear met it midway. Even with one arm trapped, she was trying to fight! Her weapon's point pierced the Beast's scales and sent him whipping back. Narga shrieked in pain.

"Thank you!" said Will. *She saved my life…but unless Sepron comes soon, we'll both be dead.*

From the Beast's back, Maximus scowled. "Kill them, Narga!" he bellowed. "Cut them to pieces!"

Will ducked as the sickle slashed at him.

"Here, use this!" said Evan, handing him her shield. Will raised it just in time to catch another bone-shaking blow. He countered with his trident, pricking the Beast's tail. *We can't keep this up for long…*

As the Beast drew away for another

attack, Will saw Ria cast her cloak
aside.

"Let me deal with him," she said.
"Even with a Beast to help you,
you're pathetic, Maximus."

She leapt towards them. Her red
hair flowed like fire under her helmet
as she drew a sword from her side.
Its blade was serrated with what
looked like a double row of uneven
sharks' teeth. She brought it down
in a vertical swipe, and Will raised
his shield. The teeth bit deep into
the wood, sending a wave of pain
through his shoulder.

Will gritted his teeth and pushed
her away. She swished the sword
through the water in dizzying arcs,
then launched another attack. Will
defended himself with his trident,
catching the blade in the prongs and

twisting it out of Ria's hand. Her eyes
narrowed with hate.

"Not bad," she said, swimming to
fetch her sword. "But you look tired."

Pain lanced through Will's shoulder
where the sickle tail had cut him, but
he adjusted his grip on the trident and
pointed it at Ria. "Try me."

Ria looked uncertainly up at Maximus. "Let's take him together," she said. "It's time to end this."

Maximus grinned, and drool fell from Narga's many sets of jaws.

"He's hungry," said Maximus. "Avantians are his favourite delicacy. Feeding time, Narga!"

ROOAAARRRR!

A sound shook the cavern, and
Will almost dropped his trident.
Sepron swept through the water,
bubbles streaming from his teeth
and his ferocious snarls filling the
cave. The Good Beast ploughed into
Narga's chest, and drove him into

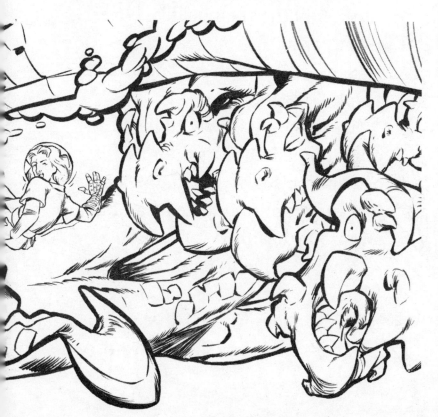

the chamber wall. Six roars escaped from Narga's throats and Will saw Maximus clinging desperately to his back. Ria, her face pale with fear, backed off beneath the safety of the arch.

Will thrust his trident back into the clam's hinge and pushed it back and forth. Still the shell held fast over Evan's arm.

"Sepron!" he called. "I need your help!"

The sea serpent twisted his head and dropped towards them. With a snap of his jaws, the clam's shell was broken into fragments and Evan swam free again.

"Now it's time to fight back," said Will.

"Finish Sepron!" yelled Maximus. Narga's six heads shot forward.

Each of his necks wrapped around
Sepron's body like an octopus's
tentacles, and his teeth sank into

Sepron's flesh. Will looked on in horror. *Surely the Evil Beast won't get the better of the mighty sea serpent...*

Sepron opened his jaws in another roar and clamped them over Narga's belly. With a jerk, he ripped the Evil Beast free and tossed him through the cavern roof into open water.

"Go, Sepron!" shouted Evan.

Will gripped Sepron's scales and pulled himself onto the Good Beast's back. He held a hand out to Evan, who joined him. Blood was leaking from puncture wounds in the sea serpent's flanks, but Sepron didn't seem to notice. His eyes shone bright and green, nostrils flaring. Will laid his gauntlet on the Beast's neck.

"After Narga!" he cried. "To battle!"

Sepron flicked his huge tail, beating the seabed and throwing clams in all directions. With a thrust of his huge body, he rose up out of the cave.

CHAPTER FOUR

SHARK ATTACK

They'd just emerged into open
water when a dark shape descended
on them. But this was no Beast.
Thousands of fish, all species and sizes,
swarmed over Sepron's body, tangling
with Will's hair and clothes. He tried
to brush them away, but more kept
coming. He felt a nip at his ankle, and
another on his neck. Squid latched
themselves onto Sepron's scales.

"They're attacking!" said Evan.

Sepron veered one way then the other, but couldn't throw the shoals off. Will felt an eel slip under his tunic, and over his back. Twisting, he grabbed its tail to pull it out. His trident was useless against so many small foes. He felt another bite, and Evan writhed behind him and cried out. He sensed Sepron's sadness that innocent creatures of the sea were joining the fight for Evil. A shoal of red jellyfish were floating towards him. *They have nasty stings…*

"They must be under Narga's control," said Will. "We mustn't hurt them."

"We need to get clear," said Evan.

Sepron put on a burst of speed, and left the shoal behind, but the dozens of fish gave chase.

"Will, look out!" said Evan.

From among a glittering shoal of mackerel, a hammerhead shark was nosing forward, its head swaying from side to side, and its eyes fixed on Will and Evan.

The shark surged towards them, eyes rolling madly. Sepron flicked his tail

and batted the shark aside. It swam
off, reeling. But another took its place.
Then there were two, then three.

This doesn't look good, thought Will. *We
should be tackling Narga, not wasting our
time on sharks.*

Sepron turned his head to snap at
the sharks, and whacked two more

out of the way with ease. But the third slipped deftly under his club-like tail and made for Will and Evan. The shark's jaws parted to reveal pink gums lined with jagged, uneven teeth. Its enchanted eyes glinted like silver coins.

Sepron tried again to knock it out of

the way, but the shark quickly veered
aside. With a sudden lunge it headed
for Evan and snapped its jaws closed.
She managed to bash its nose with
her shield just in time, and its teeth
snagged on her leg. Evan cried out as
the shark backed off.

"Are you all right?" asked Will.

She nodded, pale and shaken. "It just tore my clothes," she said.

The shark looped around to come at them again. Though Sepron was speeding through the water, the shark kept pace with powerful thrusts of its tail. Another shoal of sardines, hundreds strong, was zipping towards them from below.

"That shark will not give up," said Will. "I've got an idea."

He rolled off Sepron's back and slipped beneath the Beast's scaly belly, out of sight of the shark. He tugged his net free from his belt, and waited. It might not be strong enough to snare a Beast, but he was confident it could contain a shark. The sardines switched and twitched around him, further concealing him from the shark's view.

As the shark shot towards Evan,
Will plunged through the blurring
silver fish and threw the net just as
Elenna had showed him. It fell across
the shark's wide head, snaring the
predator. Will was tugged after it,

but he held on. The shark writhed in the net, getting more tangled, and snapped harmlessly at the metal strands.

"You're trapped!" Will said, bringing the point of his trident to bear on the shark. "Give up."

He did not know if the shark had understood his words, or was simply tired, but it stopped thrashing and struggling. The silvery sheen faded from its eyes, leaving them bewildered and afraid.

Maybe Maximus's enchantment is breaking, thought Will.

He kept a firm grip on his trident, just in case, and pulled the net from the shark's head. It shrank back, then twisted around and swam away.

"Good work," said Evan. "Oh! Will, look at that!"

More and more sharks were coming
– a dozen sleek predators nosing from
the depths. Will kicked back towards
where Sepron waited, surrounded
by swarming fish. He used his net to
drag a few aside and climb back onto
the sea serpent. Above them, he saw
the telltale shape of Narga's sickle tail,
near the surface.

"After him!" Will yelled.

Sepron left the shoals of fish behind
and climbed through the water after
Maximus's Beast. Will spied Maximus
gripping one neck and Ria astride
another.

Sepron made straight for Narga, a
low snarl coming from his throat.

As they closed to thirty paces,
Maximus lifted his whip to strike and
Ria drew her serrated blade. Sepron
did not slow down. His jaws opened

wide. *This is it*, thought Will. *There's no going back now. It might be our last chance of victory.*

But when they drew within five paces, Will saw Maximus lash his whip-leashes across Narga's necks. The Evil Beast roared and sped away in

a trail of bubbles. Unable to stop or turn, Sepron shot past where their foes had been, breaking through the sea's surface. For a moment, they were airborne, gliding over the waves, then they crashed beneath the water again.

By the time they were back underwater, Maximus had put some distance between them. "Catch us if you can!" he shouted.

"That's odd," said Evan. "I thought Maximus *wanted* the two Beasts to fight."

Will clenched his gauntleted fist. "He must be laying a trap for us."

"What shall we do?" asked Evan.

Will thought back to his father's cry as the water snatched him, and took only a heartbeat to decide. He had to follow his instincts.

"Now isn't the time to hold back," he said. "We go after Maximus, and we fight him to the finish."

CHAPTER FIVE

FIGHTING ON

Narga was almost as fast as Sepron, cutting through the underwater currents like an arrow. Sepron's crest flattened against his body as he raced in pursuit, and Will clung close to his back. "I wonder how Tom defeated Narga the first time, in Gorgonia," Will shouted over the rush of water.

"When I fought Amictus," said Evan, "I had to break Maximus's connection with the Beast."

Will pondered for a moment. "There's a difference though," he said. "Amictus was a *Good* Beast, enchanted under Maximus's spell. Narga is Evil through and through. We need to vanquish him."

"But how?" asked Evan. "It's like facing six Beasts at once!"

"Maybe we can even those odds by removing some of his heads," said Will.

They plunged into the depths, and Will realised they were closing in on their enemies. Narga seemed to have slowed near a boulder field on the ocean floor, his six heads swaying like giant cobras ready to strike.

Will commanded Sepron to slow down as well, and paused at a safe distance. He wasn't going to get caught out like last time and ram straight into the seabed. Ria leapt off Narga's neck and took another glass flask from inside her cloak. The potion inside this one was black. As she eased out the cork, the oily liquid poured out into the water and began to spiral upwards. The swirls of black spun faster and faster, growing outwards all the time like a watery tornado. Some

of the smaller rocks from the seabed were torn free and sucked into the whirlpool too.

With her cloak whipping back and forth, Ria leapt onto the Evil Beast beside Maximus. Narga carried them away a safe distance from the swirling water. Will had seen whirlpools before, in the stormy seas around Shipton, but those were tiny things. This magical spinning column would easily swallow Freya's huge ship whole.

Maximus's laughter filled the water. "Just how confident are you in your Beast?" he shouted. "One wrong move and you'll be sucked in and torn to pieces."

Ria moved her arms as if she were shaping something in the water, and the column suddenly edged nearer to Sepron. Will felt its tug, but the Good

Beast backed off just in time.

So Ria can make the whirlpool move…

"Don't get too close!" laughed Maximus.

The whirlpool lurched again, and Sepron twisted away. Too slow! The powerful current snatched at his tail. "It's got us!" yelled Evan.

For a moment, the Beast fought against the pull, then the spinning water sucked them further in. "Swim harder!" yelled Will. Sepron roared and strained and tore free.

Will guided Sepron around the edge of the column, keeping one eye on Ria. "We need to get closer to him," he muttered. But each time he thought he saw a way through to Narga, the swirling water blocked his path.

"Give up," said Ria. "You and your pathetic friend are no match for us."

"Yes, swim back to Tom and his mother with your tail between your legs," said Maximus.

"You'll have to do better than that," Will yelled back. "We're not going to the surface until Narga is vanquished."

The Evil Beast suddenly shot around the edge of the whirlpool. A mouth full of deadly teeth lurched towards them, and Will ducked as a set of jaws snapped just where his head had been.

"Aim for his teeth!" he shouted to Evan.

As the next head darted forward, she swung her shield and caught the Beast in the mouth. Narga screeched as one of his teeth broke, spinning off into the water. The Evil Beast twisted away, but lashed out with his sickle tail, slashing it across Sepron's belly. The sea serpent roared in pain.

"Good work, Narga!" said Maximus. "Soon the sea will belong to us!"

But Will could sense Sepron was more angry than hurt. *Play injured*, he said with his mind.

Sepron must have understood, because he let his crest sag and his eyelids droop. He throat gave out a low, keening sound. "He must be

badly wounded," Evan gasped.

"Finish him!" shouted Ria.

Maximus was grinning cruelly as he urged Narga towards them. All six heads were open-mouthed and drooling. As the first launched at Sepron's neck, Will stabbed with his trident. The prongs pierced one of Narga's throats, and the ugly face twisted with a strangled cry.

Will twisted his trident, and severed the head completely. It sank to the seabed, mouth still gaping and trailing green blood.

"One down, five to go," muttered Will.

He drew back his trident, dripping gore.

"Will!" said Evan. "Oh no!"

She was pointing at the stump of Narga's severed neck, where the skin was stretching and *growing*.

Two more heads sprouted from the wounds.

"One down, *seven* to go," laughed Maximus. "Another little side effect of Ria's magic."

"Impressive, eh?" said Ria.

The two new heads lunged at Will. He smacked both aside with his trident, but he didn't dare try to cut them off – he didn't want four more to grow back!

The two new heads swayed from side to side, and Will noticed that their eyes were not red like the others, but a sickly shade of yellow.

"First we'll kill Sepron," said Maximus. "Then we'll take our time with you two."

Ria's whirlpool spun close and Sepron banked away. Narga followed, heads snapping. One closed on the green crest along Sepron's back, two more on his tail. In the tangle, two heads bumped into each other, then locked eyes. They snarled as if facing an enemy, releasing Sepron's tail and darting at another of Narga's heads. Bubbles filled the water as the heads struck out at each other, roaring and biting.

Will saw Maximus yanking on his leashes, trying to control them.

"Stop that!" he urged. "*Sepron* is your enemy."

The heads finally broke apart, but their necks were covered with scars from the attack.

"What's wrong with him?" Maximus said to Ria.

The witch scowled. "You have to be firmer, that's all," she said.

She waved her hands and the spinning whirlpool jerked towards Sepron. Will felt the water's pull again, but the sea serpent fought free.

Narga's heads were scrapping amongst themselves again as Maximus struggled with the leashes.

If the Beast's new heads do battle with the old ones, Will thought, *maybe not all is lost. Perhaps we can make Narga destroy himself!*

CHAPTER SIX

SUCKED IN!

"I have a plan!" Will said to Evan.

Sepron, to the whirlpool…

The sea serpent edged nearer to the spinning column of water.

"What are you doing?" asked Evan. "We'll be sucked in!"

Will's knuckles were white where he gripped Sepron's scales. "Not all of us," he said. "Trust me."

When they were just an arm's

length from the whirlpool, Will could feel it trying to grip him again. Sepron was obviously wary, because he wouldn't go any closer. *He must be getting weaker*, thought Will. *I hope I haven't made a mistake.*

"It's got them!" Ria cheered.

Will let his body slide off Sepron's back. The current snatched him into the spinning water. He could hardly

see what was happening as the water threw him around and around. He caught glimpses of Evan's shocked face as she clung to Sepron, and the blur of Narga's heads as they whipped past.

"Kill him, Narga!" Maximus yelled.

The many-headed Beast pressed on into the whirlpool too, his necks straining against the current.

"Make it spin faster!" Maximus shouted.

As the water flung his limbs around, Will saw Ria releasing more of the black liquid into the spinning column. The whirlpool picked up speed and soon it was all he could do just to hold onto his trident.

One of Narga's heads was suddenly next to him, red eyes blazing and teeth gaping wide. Will slashed with

his trident and took off the head, sending it spinning into the depths of the whirlpool. Another head attacked and again he sliced it off. Four more heads grew to replace them, and Will lost count. *Are there nine heads or ten?*

Maximus roared at his Beast: "Tear him apart!"

The whirlpool might do that first, thought Will, as the water tossed him around and around. Sometimes he was at the centre of the column, other times he found himself at the edges. He bashed against Narga's slimy flesh, and almost fell headfirst into a set of jaws, but the water had them both in its grip.

None of the eyes, yellow or red, seemed to be watching Will now. It was time to get out of this whirlpool.

Sepron, come to me – I need your help.

Everything was a blur, but Will made out Narga's new heads turning on the old ones. He saw jaws locking around necks, heads butting into one another, necks tangling into knots and flecks of green blood trailing spirals in the water. He glimpsed Maximus's face, red with fury and dismay, as Narga wrestled with himself.

"No!" bellowed Malvel's son. "No, no, no!"

Something closed over Will's arm, and he let out a gasp. It was a hand. Evan! Hanging off Sepron's back, with her teeth gritted, she heaved him back into open water.

"Thank you!" Will gasped. His head was still spinning as he watched Narga being spun round. His eyes were wide with shock, like burning fires in the swirling water. Every few turns, a head would break loose of the current and strain to free itself, only to be sucked back in.

"Make it stop!" begged Maximus. "Please, make it stop!"

Ria was waving her arms, but the whirlpool only quickened. "I can't!" she yelled. "The magic's taken over!"

Narga was just a blur of green. Will couldn't see the Beast's body or his heads clearly any more. Maximus's cries were lost in the roar of the water, and Ria was edging away behind a large boulder.

"I think we should get clear too," said Evan.

Sepron backed off from the swelling whirlpool.

"Help meeeeee!" shouted Maximus. Will thought he glimpsed him

clutching one of Narga's necks, his eyes
wide with fear.

"You'll have to let go of the Beast!"
cried Ria.

Suddenly Maximus's body flew out of
the whirlpool, bouncing off the seabed.

BOOM!

With a deafening sound, the whirlpool

collapsed in on itself, throwing up a cloud of bubbles and sand. Will threw his hand over his face. When he pulled it away, Narga had vanished.

"We did it!" he cried, patting Sepron's neck. "We defeated the Evil Beast!"

Maximus dragged himself to his feet, clutching his neck. "I...can't...breathe!" he hissed.

Will saw that the magical explosion had cracked the bubble Maximus had used to breathe, and water was now leaking through. The level was rising over his chin. "Don't leave—"

Maximus's voice trailed off into a watery gurgle as the helmet vanished completely. Will looked around for Ria, expecting her to cast a spell to help her accomplice. He swam to the boulder she had been hiding behind, trident at the ready.

"Ria's gone!" he called to Evan.

Maximus pushed off the seabed, clawing desperately towards the surface.

"He won't make it," said Evan.

Sure enough, Maximus's limbs began to move sluggishly in the water.

I can't let him drown, thought Will. *That's not a hero's way.*

"Sepron, let's help him," he said aloud.

With a flick of his powerful tail, Sepron shot upwards. Will untucked his net and hurled it over Maximus's flailing arms. He yanked his enemy along with them as Sepron swam towards the surface.

As they broke through the waves, Evan helped haul the limp Maximus

up onto the Good Beast's neck. Will
thumped the young wizard's back to
try to get him breathing. Maximus's
face and lips were grey, his black hair
plastered to his forehead. His eyes
were closed.

"Are we too late?" muttered Evan.

Will put his fingers to Maximus's
neck to feel for a pulse. "I don't kn—"

Maximus's head jerked and he

169

spat out a mouthful of sea water. He gave a series of hacking coughs that seemed to shake his whole body.

"Are you all right?" asked Will.

Maximus rolled onto his side, gasping. "I...think so."

"You nearly drowned," said Will, laying a hand on his enemy's back.

Maximus's fist came up so quickly that Will couldn't react. The blow caught him full in the jaw and he toppled backwards.

Maximus leapt to his feet. "You should have left me down there, you weak fool!" he sneered. "I'll have my revenge, and it will be sweet!"

Evan climbed to her feet as well, brandishing her spear. "That's enough. You're outnumbered. Surrender!"

"Never!" said Maximus. "This isn't

over. I'll be back, with more Beasts than you can handle!"

In flash of black sparks, he disappeared.

Will sat up, rubbing his jaw. "He got away," he sighed.

"That doesn't matter," said Evan. "You defeated the Evil Beast. Your Quest is over."

"Not quite," said Will after a moment's pause. "I've got an idea how we can stop Maximus from raising any more Beasts."

Evan raised one of her eyebrows. "How?"

Will pointed back into the water. "By destroying his magical lair."

CHAPTER SEVEN

CELEBRATION

Under the water, life had returned to
normal. Shoals of brightly coloured
fish glided through the depths, no
longer under Narga's spell. A group
of sharks nosed between the seaweed
beds, and rays hovered over the ocean
floor to search for their prey. Sepron
carried Will and Evan back towards
the dome where Maximus and Ria
had been hatching their evil plans.

"We should be careful," said Will. "Ria might be waiting for us inside."

He clutched his trident in one hand.

But when they reached the site of the underwater lair, it was empty. The only sign it had ever been there was the field of giant clams.

"This must be the spot," said Evan, frowning. "How can they have moved the whole lair?"

"Dark magic," Will muttered angrily. He tried to put his disappointment aside. "We need to tell Tom and Elenna that the Knights-in-Training haven't seen the last of Maximus."

He was about to direct Sepron back to the surface, when the glint of silver caught his eye. "Wait a moment," he said, slipping off the Beast's back.

He swam in the direction of the curious glint, finding Freya's bone-

handled dagger half buried in the sand. He smiled as he plucked it out and tucked it into his belt.

Sepron brought them up right in the middle of the fleet of boats. Freya's barge still rocked in the water beside them, but she had joined Tom on his boat. A wave rolled off the sea serpent's back, making all the vessels rock on the swell. Will tried not to

chuckle as he saw Seb almost stumble overboard. The rest of the recruits were backing away to the edge of the boat as Sepron glared at them with his enormous eyes.

"Don't worry," said Tom, leaning off his boat to stroke the great sea serpent's nose. "He won't do us any harm."

"We were starting to wonder where

you were!" said Elenna.

The ruby in Tom's belt glowed. He nodded, smiling at Sepron. Will had heard that the red jewel allowed Tom to communicate directly with Beasts, Good or Evil.

"Sepron tells me you both showed great courage in vanquishing Narga," said Tom, as he helped Will and Evan into the boat beside him.

Will felt blood rush to his cheeks. "We couldn't have done it without Sepron," he said.

The Sea Serpent blew a mouthful of spray across the decks of the boats, soaking everyone.

"Urgh," said Seb. "That's disgusting!"

But Tom was laughing, and the rest of the young knights joined in.

Will drew the dagger from his belt

and held it out to Freya. She smiled, then shook her head. "It belongs to you now."

"I...I can't accept—" said Will.

"Only a true hero could have brought it back from the depths of the ocean," she said. "Please, keep it as a reminder of your Quest."

Will bowed to Gwildor's Mistress of the Beasts, and tucked the dagger away, his face flushing again – but with pride now.

"Elenna was right," he said. "Maximus *does* have a lair. But he's got a helper too. A girl called Ria. She—"

Tom held up his hand. "You two should rest, for now," he said. "We'll talk more back at King Hugo's castle. Our enemies can wait."

Will nodded. The golden gauntlet

felt suddenly heavy on his hand. It slipped off, clattering into the bottom of the boat. "Your Quest is over," said Daltec. He stooped to retrieve the gauntlet and slipped it inside his robes.

Freya crossed her boat and whispered in the Wizard's ear. Daltec's face broke into a grin. "Good idea!" he said. "A celebration is just what we need."

With a wave of his hand, sparks flashed across Freya's boat, and when they disappeared, banners and streamers flew from the masts. The decks groaned with food-laden tables.

"A feast for all!" said Freya. "To celebrate our new heroes, Will and Evan!"

"To Will and Evan!" they all cried.

Sepron blasted another spurt of seawater over the boat.

"And Sepron!" said Will.

The sea serpent rose up above the waves, then dipped his head and plunged beneath the water. The long curl of his tail followed, leaving only white foam on the surface. Will's heart swelled with pride.

As the other recruits were climbing aboard Freya's boat, Tom fell in beside Will. "You saved the kingdom today," he said. "Your father would be proud of you."

Will took a sharp breath. "My father... He's—"

"I know," said Tom. "I've heard all about it."

Will felt his cheeks flush. "Who told you? I didn't think anyone outside Shipton knew."

Tom smiled warmly. "I've known since I first selected you to join the other Knights-in-Training. It's *why* I selected you. The trader who brings fish to the castle told me your story. He said you dived deeper than

anyone thought possible, to rescue your father."

Will lowered his eyes. "It was my fault," he said. "If I had—"

Tom gripped his shoulder. "Listen, Will, accidents will always happen. You've proved today that you don't lack for courage."

"What are you two waiting for?" Elenna called from the other ship. Silver was already gnawing on a chicken drumstick.

"Forget the past," said Tom. "It's the future that matters."

"The future." Will nodded, and his heart felt lighter than it had in a very long time.

Tom leapt on board Freya's ship. "For now, we celebrate," he shouted, his eyes travelling to each of the recruits. "But be warned, Knights-

in-Training… Evil *never* sleeps.
Maximus will come again! Avantia
will need a new hero soon!"

JOIN TOM ON HIS NEXT
BEAST QUEST SOON!

Join the Quest,
Join the Tribe

www.beastquest.co.uk

Have you checked out the Beast Quest website?
It's the place to go for games, downloads, activities,
sneak previews and lots of fun!

You can read all about your favourite Beasts, down-
load free screensavers and desktop wallpapers for
your computer, and even challenge your friends
to a Beast Tournament.

Sign up to the newsletter at www.beastquest.co.uk
to receive exclusive extra content and the opportunity to enter special members-only competitions.
We'll send you up-to-date info on all the Beast
Quest books, including the next exciting series
which features six brand-new Beasts!

Get 30% off all Beast Quest Books at www.beastquest.co.uk
Enter the code BEAST at the checkout.

FROM THE DARK, A HERO ARISES...

Dare to enter the kingdom of Avantia.

A new evil arises in Avantia. Lord Derthsin has ordered his armies into the four corners of Avantia. If the four Beasts of Avantia can find their Chosen Riders they might have the strength to challenge Derthsin. But if they fail, the land of Avantia will be lost forever...

FIRST HERO, CHASING EVIL
CALL TO WAR, FIRE AND FURY-
OUT NOW!

All books priced at £4.99.
Special bumper editions priced at £5.99.

Orchard Books are available from all good bookshops, or can be ordered from our website: www.orchardbooks.co.uk, or telephone 01235 827702, or fax 01235 8227703.

Series 12: THE DARKEST HOUR
COLLECT THEM ALL!

Three lands are in terrible danger from six new Beasts. Tom must ride to the rescue!

978 1 40832 396 0

978 1 40832 397 7

978 1 40832 398 4

978 1 40832 399 1

978 1 40832 400 4

978 1 40832 401 1

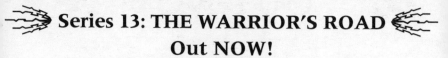

Join Tom on his Beast Quests
and take part in a terrifying adventure
where YOU call the shots!

LOOK OUT FOR SERIES 2:

THE CAVERN OF GHOSTS

OUT SEPTEMBER 2013

978 1 40832 411 0   978 1 40832 412 7   978 1 40832 413 4   978 1 40832 414 1

978 1 40831 852 2

COMING SOON!

SPECIAL BUMPER EDITION

FREE COLLECTOR CARDS INSIDE!